Don Quixote and the Windmills

QUIXOTE

RETOLD AND ADAPTED BY Eric A. Kimmel

FROM The Ingenious Hidalgo Don Quixote de la Mancha
BY Miguel de Cervantes Saavedra

PICTURES BY Leonard Everett Fisher

FARRAR, STRAUS AND GIROUX • NEW YORK

Are you one who loves old stories? Does your heart beat faster when you hear tales of knights in armor? Of castles and dragons? Of ogres, sorcerers, and damsels in distress? Beware! Those tales can drive you mad. It happened to a certain Spanish gentleman who lived four centuries ago in the province of La Mancha.

Señor Quexada was his name. He had a tall, lean figure and wore a woeful expression on his face, as if his heart held some secret sorrow.

Indeed, it did. Señor Quexada longed to live in days gone by, when gallant knights battled for the honor of ladies fair. Books of their adventures filled his library. *Amadis of Gaul*, *The Mirror of Chivalry*, and *The Exploits of Esplandián* were but a few of the volumes that tumbled from his shelves.

Señor Quexada buried himself in these books. He read all day and far into the night, until his mind snapped. "Señor Quexada is no more," he announced to his astonished household. "I am the renowned knight and champion Don Quixote de la Mancha."

In the attic he found a rusty suit of armor, his grandfather's sword, a round leather shield, and an antique lance. His helmet was a foot soldier's steel cap that lacked a visor. Don Quixote made one out of paperboard and tied it on with ribbons. It would serve until he won himself a proper helmet on the field of battle.

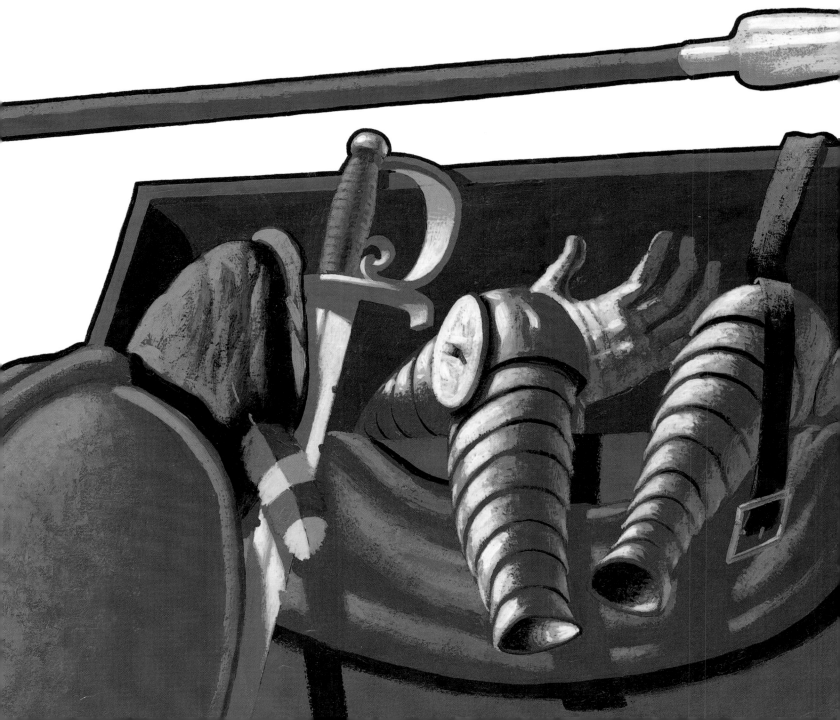

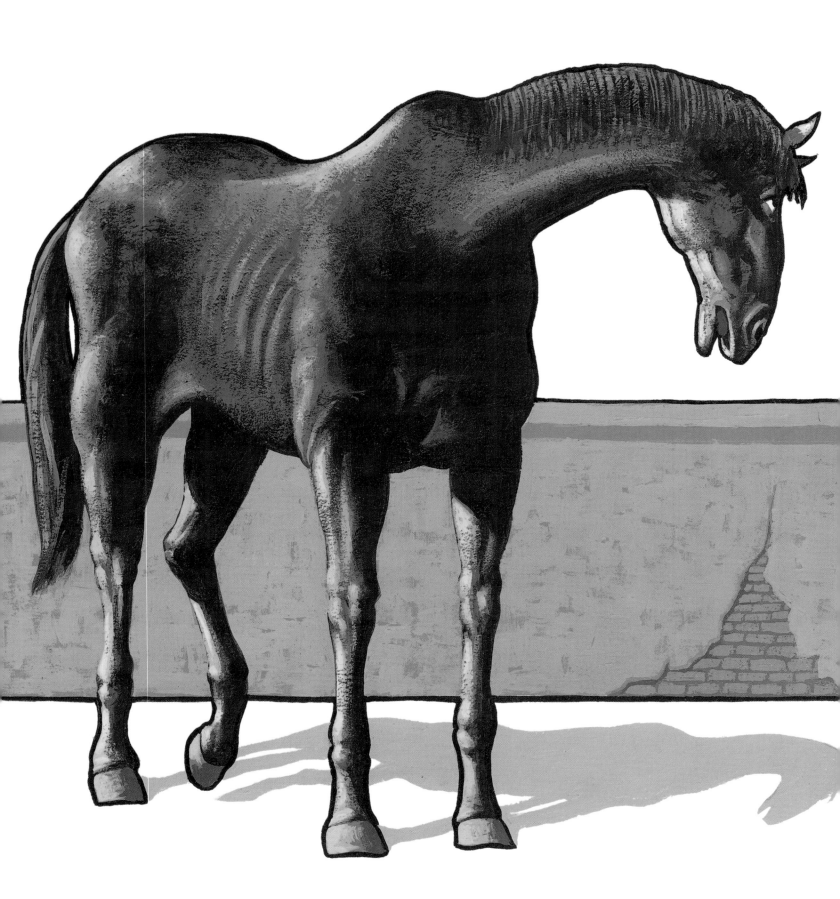

A knight must have a noble steed. Don Quixote owned a nag as tall and bony as himself. He named the horse Rocinante, which means "Nag No More."

A knight must also have a squire, a faithful companion to share his quests. Don Quixote invited Sancho Panza, a short, fat farmer from the neighborhood, to accompany him. "Come with me, Sancho," Don Quixote said. "Within a week I will conquer an island and make you king of it."

"That will be no bad thing," Sancho replied. "If I were king of an island, my wife would be queen, and all my children princes and princesses." So Sancho agreed to come along. Although he was not as crackbrained as Don Quixote, he certainly saw no harm in seeing a bit of the world.

Finally, a knight must have a fair lady to whom he has pledged his loyalty and his life. "A knight without a lady is like a tree without leaves or fruit, a body without a soul," Don Quixote explained to Sancho. After considering all the damsels in the district, he chose a pretty farm girl—Aldonza Lorenzo—from the village of Toboso.

Don Quixote rechristened his lady as he had rechristened his horse. He called her "Dulcinea," meaning "Sweetness." The very word breathed music and enchantment.

"Dulcinea of Toboso . . . Dulcinea . . . Dulcinea . . ." The knight's heart overflowed with devotion as he whispered the sacred name.

One moonless night, while everyone in town lay asleep, Don Quixote and Sancho set forth. By dawn they were miles away. Don Quixote rode ahead, scanning the plain for ogres and sorcerers. Sancho followed on his little donkey, munching his breakfast of bread and cheese.

Don Quixote halted. "Fortune has favored our quest, good Sancho. Can you see what lies yonder? There stand the monstrous giants who have plagued this countryside long enough. I intend to strike them down and claim their wealth as our just reward."

Sancho squinted into the distance. "Giants, Master? What are you talking about? I see no giants."

"There they are. Straight ahead. Can't you see them? They have four arms, each one more than six miles long."

"Oh, Master, you are mistaken. Those aren't giants. They're windmills. What you call arms are really sails to catch the wind. The wind turns the sails and makes the millstones go round and round."

"It is plain you know nothing at all," Don Quixote replied. "I say those are giants, whether or not you recognize them as such. I intend to slay them. If you are frightened, you may hide yourself away and say your prayers while I challenge them to mortal combat."

Having said this, Don Quixote lowered his visor and put his spurs to Rocinante. He galloped across the plain to do battle with the windmills.

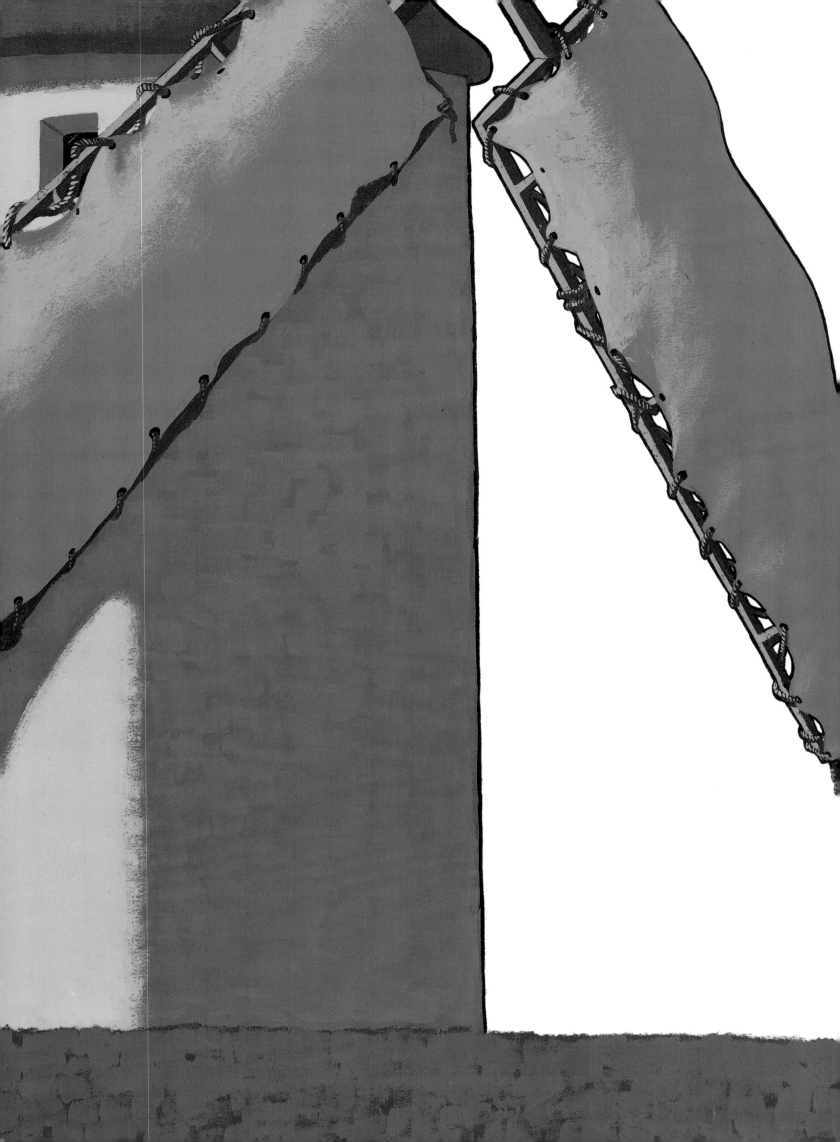

"Take to your heels, cowardly giants! Know that it is I, the noble Don Quixote, Knight of La Mancha, who am attacking you!"

"Master! They are only windmills!" Sancho called after him.

The wind picked up. The sails billowed. The great arms of the windmills began to turn.

Don Quixote laughed with scorn. "Do you think to frighten me? Though you have more arms than the giant Briareus, I will still make an end of you!" He lifted his eyes toward heaven. "Beautiful damsel, Dulcinea of Toboso, in your honor do I claim the victory. If I am to die, let it be with your sweet name upon my lips."

Shouting defiance, he charged at the nearest windmill.

His lance pierced the canvas sail and became tangled in the ropes. Attempting to pull free, Don Quixote became caught as well. The windmill's rumbling arm dragged him out of the saddle, carrying him higher and higher.

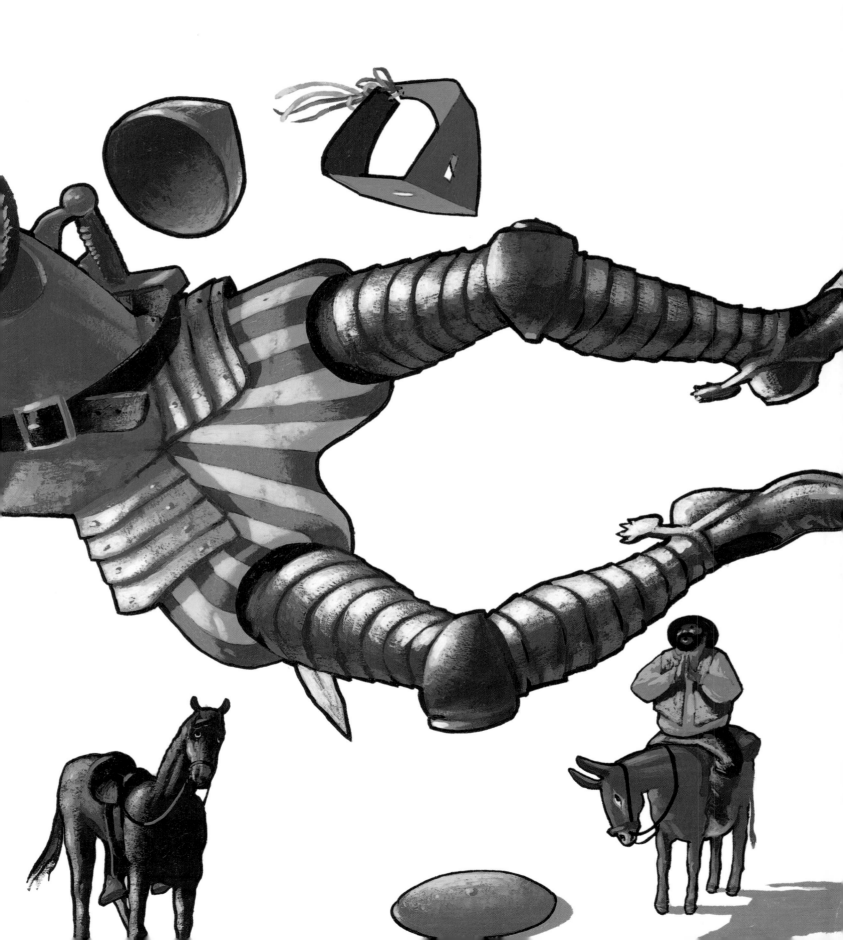

Don Quixote drew his sword. "Release me, Giant, before you feel the sharp sting of my blade!" He slashed at the ropes. The windmill's arm swept past its zenith. It began hurtling toward the ground at an ever-increasing speed.

Sancho trotted up on his donkey. "Master, I will save you!" He grasped Don Quixote's ankle when the knight swept by. The faithful squire found himself pulled off his donkey and carried aloft with his master.

"Do not fear, good Sancho. I feel the giant weakening. I will soon make an end of this villain." Don Quixote hacked at the ropes with renewed vigor.

Sancho saw the cords begin to fray. "Master! Spare the poor giant a few moments of life. At least until he brings us closer to the ground."

"Giant, in the name of my lady, Dulcinea of Toboso, I command you to yield or die."

Don Quixote made one last thrust. The ropes parted. The sail blew away. Don Quixote, with Sancho clinging to his ankle, plunged straight down. Together they would have perished, knight and squire, dashed to a hundred pieces, had the sail of the following arm not caught them and sent them rolling across the plain.

They tumbled to a stop at Rocinante's feet. Sancho felt himself all over for broken bones. "Ay, Master!" he groaned. "Why didn't you listen to me? I tried to warn you. Could you not see that they were only windmills? Whatever possessed you to attack them?"

Don Quixote dusted off his battered armor. He tied the crushed visor back onto his helmet. "Be silent, Sancho. Your words reveal your ignorance. You know nothing about these matters. It is true that the giants now have the appearance of windmills. This is because they were bewitched by my enemy, the wizard Frestón. At the last moment, he transformed the giants into windmills to deprive me of the glorious victory that was rightfully mine. Never fear, Sancho. We will meet him again. All the power of his magic arts will not save him when he feels the edge of my mighty sword."

"I hope so," said Sancho as he pushed Don Quixote back onto Rocinante. "Another tumble like this and we will all go home in pieces."

Don Quixote took the reins in hand. "Never fear, faithful Sancho. The road to victory is often paved with misfortune. A true knight never complains. Follow me, and I promise we will dip our arms up to the elbow in what common people call 'adventures.' Our names and the stories of our matchless deeds will resound through the ages."

"Ay, Master! When I hear you say those words, I can almost believe they are true. Perhaps I really will have my island someday."

"Of course you will, Sancho. Why would you ever doubt it?"

Sancho mounted his donkey and went trotting after Rocinante, vowing to follow Don Quixote wherever fortune's winds might carry him.

Author's Note

The Ingenious Hidalgo Don Quixote de la Mancha is one of the greatest works of Spanish literature. Its author, Miguel de Cervantes Saavedra (1547–1616), had as many adventures—and suffered as many disasters—as his hero, Don Quixote.

Cervantes began his career as a soldier. He fought and was severely wounded at the great sea battle of Lepanto in 1571. Captured by pirates and sold as a slave in Algiers, he did not return to Spain until 1580.

Cervantes had no more luck as a civilian than he'd had as a soldier. Having obtained a job as a tax collector in order to pay his bills, he landed in jail when officials questioned his accounts. The idea for Don Quixote came to him while he was imprisoned in Seville's dungeon.

Don Quixote was published in 1605 and became an instant success. Readers demanded a sequel, which appeared in 1615. Cervantes died in Madrid the following year, at the height of his fame.

Don Quixote's battle with the windmills has remained one of the most enduring images in world literature for four hundred years. It has given us the expression "tilting at windmills," which means recklessly charging out to do battle with an imaginary enemy.

To my new grandson, Blake Andrew Oren —E.A.K.

For my grandchildren: Lauren, Michael, Samuel, Jordan, Gregory, and Danielle
— L.E.F.

Copyright © 2004 by Shearwater Books
Illustrations copyright © 2004 by Leonard Everett Fisher
All rights reserved
Distributed in Canada by Douglas & McIntyre Ltd.
Color separations by Hong Kong Scanner Arts
Printed and bound in the United States of America by Berryville Graphics
Designed by Robbin Gourley
First edition, 2004
1 3 5 7 9 10 8 6 4 2

Library of Congress Cataloging-in-Publication Data
Kimmel, Eric A.
  Don Quixote and the windmills / retold and adapted by Eric A. Kimmel from The
ingenious hidalgo Don Quixote de la Mancha by Miguel de Cervantes Saavedra ;
pictures by Leonard Everett Fisher.— 1st ed.
    p. cm.
  Summary: Immersed in tales of knights and dragons and sorcerers and damsels in
distress, Señor Quexada proclaims himself a knight and sets out on his first adventure
against some nearby windmills that he thinks are giants.
  ISBN 0-374-31825-5
  [1. Knights and knighthood—Fiction. 2. Spain—Fiction.] I. Fisher, Leonard Everett, ill.
II. Cervantes Saavedra, Miguel de, 1547-1616. Don Quixote. III. Title.

PZ7.K5648 Do 2004
[Fic]—dc21
                                                                        2002067172